Cara
the Coding
Fairy

by Daisy Meadows

ORCHARD

www.rainbowmagic.co.uk

The Fairyland Palace

Cara's Computer Lab

Seeing Pool

Wetherbury Village

Wetherbury City
Conference Ce

Contents

Story One:
The Lucky Laptop

Story Two:
The Crafty Calculator

Story Three:
The Nifty Notebook

Jack Frost's Spell

Goblins, time to do some coding.
Steal a laptop! Start downloading!
I don't care if you're confused.
Your leader wants to be amused.

Build me apps to spread my fame:
Jack Frost News! A Jack Frost game!
With Cara's magic I will be
The master of technology!

Story One
The Lucky Laptop

Chapter One
Professor in a Muddle

"We're here!" said Rachel Walker, undoing her seatbelt and smiling at her best friend, Kirsty Tate.

Rachel and Kirsty had been looking forward to the coding convention Funcode for weeks. The organiser, Professor Stark, was an old school friend of Mr Walker's. He had sent the girls two tickets to the convention so that they could brush up their skills and learn the latest programming methods.

"I'm sorry we're a bit late," said Mr Walker, checking his watch.

"That's OK," said Rachel. "It's easy to get lost in the city."

The best friends jumped out of Mr Walker's car and looked up at the city conference centre.

"Oh my goodness, this place is huge," said Kirsty.

"I think the whole of Wetherbury village would fit inside," said Rachel with a laugh.

"Have you got your rucksacks?" Mr Walker asked. "Laptops? Snacks?"

The girls shared an excited smile and

nodded at him.

"We've got everything, Dad," said Rachel. "This is going to be so cool."

"I'll meet you out here at the end of the day," said Mr Walker. "Have fun."

Rachel hugged her dad goodbye, and then she and Kirsty hurried up the steps into the conference centre.

"You could fit an aeroplane in this lobby," said Rachel.

The glass-domed space was packed
with stalls and stands, all with big tables
and rows of computers. Children of all
ages were milling around the stalls or
working on the computers. A signpost
stood in front of the girls, with arrows
pointing them towards the different
events, activities and stalls. Several other
children were staring up at the signpost,
looking confused.

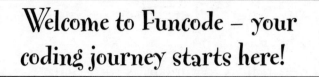

Welcome to Funcode – your coding journey starts here!

Coding for beginners 10am	Drones 10.30am
How to build a website 11am	Drop-in app class
Key coding skills 12.30pm	Design a game 1pm
Robotics skills 1.30pm	Advanced coding 2pm
How to hit your deadlines 2.30pm	

"I can't work out how to get to all the classes I want," said a girl nearby. "That list is so confusing."

"Let's go to the hub," said Rachel to

Kirsty. "That's where Professor Stark told Dad he would be."

They followed the signs and arrows, but they kept finding themselves back at the entrance. At last they ignored the arrows and walked towards the centre of the building. There they saw a circle of tables around a lectern.

"This must be the hub," said Kirsty.

The man standing at the lectern was wearing a small microphone, so the girls could hear every word he said.

"That's him," said Rachel. "That's Dad's friend Professor Stark."

The girls found some empty seats at a table and sat down to listen.

"Er, hang on," mumbled Professor Stark. "I've lost my notes again. Aha, here we are. Now, what was I saying? Yes,

welcome to, er, um, Funcode."

"Can't hear you," someone shouted.

Professor Stark dropped all his papers and kneeled down to pick them up. Just then, a teacher dashed up to the lectern with a look of panic.

"Am I teaching this class?" she demanded.

"Er, no," said Professor Stark. "You're

supposed to be on the other side of the hall."

The panicking teacher scurried away, and Professor Stark cleared his throat.

"The Funcode teachers will help you to create your own programs," he said. "You'll meet other programmers and share ideas with each other. We want you to er, um, think creatively, figure things out logically and work as a team. We're starting with Coding for Beginners. I just need to finish making a few notes. I was supposed to finish them yesterday but I, er, got confused about which day it was."

"What was the first thing you said?" asked a confused-looking little boy. "I've forgotten already."

Just then, three more children turned up

late. Professor Stark smiled at them and dropped his notes again.

"I don't think it's going very well for your dad's friend," said Kirsty.

"I can't understand it," said Rachel. "Dad told me that Professor Stark has always been really well organised and brilliant at teaching, but he seems completely muddled. What's gone wrong?"

Chapter Two
Fairy Surprise

"Er, let's take a break – er – before we start," said Professor Stark.

Rachel and Kirsty went over to a vending machine to get some water. Rachel pressed the button and reached through the slot.

"That's odd," she said, turning to Kirsty. "I didn't get a bottle."

She crouched down and peered through the slot. Then she gave a little squeak of excitement. A golden glow was coming from inside the slot. It grew brighter, and sparkles fizzed upwards.

"What is it?" asked Kirsty, bending down beside her.

"Magic," whispered Rachel.

The girls had been friends with the fairies since they had first met on Rainspell Island. From then on, they had always been ready for magical adventures.

As they watched, a tiny fairy slipped out of the slot and fluttered up to land on Rachel's hand. She was wearing polka-dotted skinny jeans and an orange jacket, and her gossamer wings were glowing.

"Hello," said Kirsty. "I'm Kirsty, and this

is Rachel."

"Hi," said the fairy, her brown eyes shining. "I'm Cara the Coding Fairy, and I'm so glad I found you. I've come to ask a huge favour. Samira the Superhero Fairy thought that you might be able to help me."

"We're always glad to help our fairy friends," said Rachel. "What's wrong?"

"Terrible news," said Cara. "Jack Frost has stolen my three magical objects."

"That mean Jack Frost is always causing trouble," said Kirsty. "Why has he taken your things?"

Just then, all the mobile phones in the convention centre started to beep. Rachel took out her mobile and gasped. A picture of Jack Frost was waving at them from the phone. A banner saying "New Jack Frost app coming soon!" scrolled across the screen.

"That's why,' said Cara. "He wants to build a complicated app all about himself."

"We have to stop him," said Rachel. "Everything's going wrong here at Funcode. I thought it would be fun, but it's just one huge muddle."

"Without my magical objects, everything to do with coding will start to go wrong," said Cara.

Kirsty glanced around to see if anyone was listening. The nearest children were trying to work out their timetables, and scratching their heads in confusion.

"Cara, please take us to Fairyland," Kirsty said. "I'm sure we can help you to find Jack Frost and get your things back."

"Let's find somewhere to hide," said Rachel. "Then

you can cast your spell."

Behind the vending machine, Cara waved her wand. At once, the chatter and buzz of the convention faded, and Rachel and Kirsty felt the prickle of magic as they shrank to fairy size. No matter how many times it happened, it was always exciting to feel their delicate wings unfold. Cara swished her wand and glittering sparkles swirled around them like a magical whirlwind.

"Let's go to Fairyland," she said with a great big smile.

Chapter Three
Goblins in the Forest

When the sparkles faded, Rachel
and Kirsty found themselves standing
in a small room with a round white
table in the centre. Six silver laptops
sat on the table.

"Welcome to my computer lab," said
Cara, twirling around. "This is where I
help other fairies learn about apps and

teach them how to code."

"You must be very busy," said Rachel.

"Yes, but I love it," said Cara. "I'm usually very good at organising my time. But since I lost my lucky laptop I've been feeling a bit muddled myself."

"What sort of apps do you design?" asked Kirsty.

"We try to think of ways to help the human world," said Cara. "Then Sabrina the Sweet Dreams Fairy helps us to give the ideas in dreams to coding experts all over the human world."

"That's amazing," said Rachel. "I had no idea that you did things like that."

"I won't ever be able to do it again if I don't get my magical objects back," said Cara sadly.

"What are your magical objects?"

Kirsty asked Cara.

"The lucky laptop helps coders do things quickly and meet their deadlines," said Cara. "The crafty calculator keeps things clear and stops coders from getting confused, and the nifty notebook helps everyone stay organised."

"How did Jack Frost get them?" asked Rachel.

Cara waved her wand, and one of the computer screens flickered on.

"I have an app that records everything that happens in this lab," she said. "Let me show you what happened in the middle of the night."

The picture on the screen showed the computer lab. The door rattled and then creaked open. Jack Frost tiptoed in, followed by three goblins. Each of them was carrying a torch.

"Start searching," Jack Frost hissed. "That fairy has things that will build me the best app ever."

The goblins bumbled around the lab, crashing into the table and opening all the cupboards.

"Got them!" screeched the tallest goblin. "I'm the winner!"

Jack Frost shoved him out of the way.

"You're not the winner," he shouted. "I'm always the winner. Give me that silly fairy's stuff right now. I'm going to hide it where she'll never find it."

He swept everything from the cupboard into a bag, and then waved his wand.

In a flash of blue lightning, Jack Frost, the goblins and Cara's magical objects vanished from the lab. The computer screen turned off.

"We have to find him and get your things back," said Kirsty. "We should fly straight to the Ice Castle and make him do the right thing."

Soon, the three fairies were swooping over clusters of toadstool houses and

sparkling blue streams.

"I've never been to Jack Frost's castle before," said Cara.

"We're getting close now," said Kirsty. "There's the forest ahead."

"The castle is just on the other side of the forest," Rachel told Cara.

Halfway across the forest, they saw snow clinging to the branches and the air grew chillier.

"Look down there," said Kirsty suddenly.

She pointed to a clearing in the middle of the forest. Two goblins were standing there, having a tug of war with something small and black.

"Let's go and see what they're doing," said Rachel. "We might be able to find out something about Jack Frost."

The fairies zoomed downwards, and landed beside a tree.

"Give it to me," the tall goblin was

yelling. "You can have the other one."

"I don't want the silly old grey one," shouted the short goblin.

"What on earth are they fighting about?" Kirsty asked.

Rachel peered at the black thing the goblins were both holding.

"It's a mouse," she said in astonishment.

"A real mouse?" Kirsty exclaimed.

"No, a computer mouse," said Cara.

"I bet they're the goblins that helped Jack Frost to steal from you," said Rachel.

"Oh, girls, I have to talk to them," said Cara urgently. "Maybe they know where Jack Frost has hidden my things."

She stepped out from behind the tree. Each of the goblins jumped backwards, and the mouse flew into the air.

"Fairies!" yelled the tall goblin.

"Run!" shouted the short goblin.
"Jack Frost told us to meet him, and we can't be late!"

They sprinted into the forest.

Chapter Four
Exploding Laptops

"We have to stop them," said Rachel.
"Come on!"

The fairies dodged between trees,
chasing the stamping feet and squawking
voices, but the noise of the goblins got
fainter and fainter.

"Which way?" asked Cara, stopping and looking left and right.

"We've lost them," said Kirsty.

They darted through the forest in the direction of the castle, listening hard, but they couldn't hear a single squawk any more. Then they reached an icy glade and stopped, shivering.

"What's this place?" said Kirsty.

A small wooden shack stood in the middle of the glade. The fairies drew closer to the shack.

"I can hear someone shouting inside," said Cara.

"Whoever it is sounds really cross," said Rachel. She exchanged a glance with her best friend.

"I think I recognise that voice," said Kirsty, her eyes wide.

They tiptoed to the shack and peered in through one icy window. Inside, they could see three goblins with laptops, and a tall figure with a spiky beard.

"Jack Frost," Rachel whispered.

"Get my castle app working by the end of the day, or else you will all be sorry," Jack Frost was yelling at the three goblins.

"I've enchanted your laptops to explode if you get it wrong, and that's not all. I'll make you drink cabbage water. I'll turn your Goblin Village huts into cardboard boxes. You have the lucky laptop in here, so with the help of its magic, you can manage to follow my orders and be the best coders ever!"

"But the lucky laptop doesn't work like that," Cara murmured. "It helps coders to meet their deadlines. It won't give the goblins coding skills."

There was a flash of blue lightning, and Jack Frost disappeared. The tallest goblin's mouth turned down.

"I don't want to be a coder," he whined. "I don't want to build an app. I just want to eat yummy stuff and laze around.

Stupid computers." He hit his laptop with one hand. "Ow!"

"Shut up, moany," grumbled the second goblin. "We have to do this by the time Jack Frost comes back."

"What are we supposed to be doing?" asked the third goblin.

"Weren't you listening?" grumbled the tallest goblin. "We have to build the part of the app that shows the Ice Castle, and we have to get it right or our laptops will explode."

"I had my fingers in my ears," said the third goblin. "Let's just start. How hard can coding be, anyway? If we type enough words and numbers, we'll get it in the end."

He started jabbing at his laptop keys, and the others copied him.

"Oh no, they have no idea about coding," said Cara.

"One of them has his eyes shut," added Kirsty.

"Is that laptop on fire?" asked Rachel.

Black smoke was curling out of the keyboard. The goblin backed away. *WIBBLE! FIZZ!* The second goblin's laptop shut itself down.

The third goblin pressed a few random keys.

"Coding is easy-peasy," he boasted. "I'll do this and Jack Frost will make me the boss of you."

The other goblins stuck their tongues
out at him, just as his laptop gave a high-
pitched squeal and exploded.

"Oh, those poor laptops," said Cara.

The tallest goblin bent down and
opened a cupboard. There was a pile of
black laptops inside, with a single pink
one on top.

"That's my lucky laptop!" Cara

exclaimed. "Without that, everyone is going to be behind on their deadlines and disorganised. I have to get it back."

Rachel thought about Professor Stark dropping his notes that morning, and frowned. She fluttered over to the door and gently tried the handle.

"It's locked," she whispered. "We have to think of a way to make the goblins come out."

"I've got an idea," said Kirsty in a low voice. "Those goblins are not enjoying coding. I bet we could distract them."

"How?" asked Rachel.

Kirsty smiled. "Goblins like games," she said. "Cara and I will get them away from the shack so that you can get in."

She rapped on the door, which opened a crack. A long green nose poked out through the crack.

"What? Go away!" he snapped. "No fairies allowed!"

Kirsty reached out and tapped the goblin on the shoulder.

"Tag!" she cried. "You're it!"

She turned and ran, pulling Rachel after her, and the goblin cackled.

"I love this game!" he yelled. "Come on, let's catch a fairy!"

Chapter Five
Jack Frost's Deadline

All three goblins raced out of the shack. Cara and Kirsty zoomed around the glade, and Rachel slipped through the open door. The lucky laptop was still inside the cupboard, and Rachel darted forwards and picked it up.

"Stop, you sneaky fairy!" shouted a voice behind her.

Rachel spun around and saw the tallest goblin glaring at her from the doorway. He slammed the door shut.

"Got you!" he yelled.

Outside, Cara and Kirsty saw the door shut and zoomed upwards. The other two goblins raced to the shack and peered through the window.

"We have to get back in there and finish the app," wailed the short goblin.

"We have to get Rachel out of there," said Kirsty.

Cara flicked her wand and the door opened. Rachel and the goblin came out, each holding on to one side of the lucky laptop.

"You have to give it back," Rachel said. "Otherwise nothing will run on time, the coding convention will be a disaster, and my dad's school friend will have failed."

"I don't care about your stupid convention," squawked the goblin. "If we don't finish Jack Frost's app, we will be late for our deadline. And Jack Frost is much scarier than your dad's friend!"

Cara and Kirsty landed behind Rachel, and the other two goblins ran up behind

the tallest goblin.

"Let go!" the goblin screeched at
Rachel. "Jack Frost said it would help
us write the code on time, and all the
other laptops have exploded because of
our mistakes."

"Listen," said Rachel. "Jack Frost is
being mean. He wants you to create
an app, even though you don't know

anything about coding. It's not fair. But Cara knows everything about coding. She could help you to make an app of Jack Frost's castle and meet your deadline – if she had the lucky laptop."

The goblins exchanged suspicious looks.

"Do you really want to keep making laptops explode?" Kirsty asked. "Wouldn't you rather have Jack Frost think you've obeyed his orders?"

The tallest goblin thought about it for a moment. Then, scowling, he shoved the lucky laptop at Rachel. She quickly turned and handed it to Cara, who hugged it to her chest.

"Thank you," she said, raising her wand.

Instantly, the broken laptops in the shack were mended. They all started pinging and an interactive picture of Jack Frost's castle appeared on the screens.

"We're geniuses!" squealed the short goblin, dashing over to the nearest screen. "Well, I am. Look what I did!"

Cara laughed and the three friends put their arms around each other.

"Thank you from the bottom of my heart," Cara said. "I'm going to send you back to the human world now, but I will follow as soon as I can. There are still two more objects to find."

"We'll be waiting for you," Rachel promised, smiling.

With a wave of Cara's wand, the girls found themselves back in the human world again, crouching down behind the vending machine. Not a single second had passed since they went to Fairyland.

"Listen," said Rachel as they walked back to the hub.

Professor Stark was talking again, but this time he sounded very different.

"I cannot wait for you all to find out the amazing things we have in store for you," he said. "Today, in our carefully

planned programme of events, you will
learn the key skills you'll need to become
the most brilliant coders of the future. All
you need is a project and a plan."

Rachel and Kirsty smiled at each other
and sat down.

"I wish we had an app that could tell
us when we're next going to see a fairy,"
whispered Rachel.

"I love learning about coding and apps," said Kirsty with a laugh. "But I'm happy for our fairy adventures to stay just the way they are!"

Story Two
The Crafty Calculator

Chapter Six
Confused Coders

Rachel and Kirsty sat down at the hub and Professor Stark smiled at them.

"You're just in time for the Funcode Challenge," he said, handing them a sheet of instructions. "I want everyone to work in pairs. This project will test your coding skills and teach you some

new ones. Use the code blocks to dress
up three pixies and make them dance
under a rainbow. Make the costumes and
dances as exciting as you can. At the end
of this hour, I'll choose a winner."

Eagerly, Rachel opened her laptop and
started to type the website address, but
she kept getting it wrong.

"Silly me, I can't seem to remember
where the letters are," she said.

"This looks like fun," said Kirsty peering over her shoulder. "Let's start with the scenery."

She used the mouse to drag a code block across the screen. Then she paused. "That's odd," she said. "I can't remember where to put it."

"Are you Rachel and Kirsty?" asked Professor Stark. "Your dad said that you'd be here today, Rachel. Welcome to Funcode. Are you enjoying it?"

"It's been even more exciting than we expected," said Kirsty, sharing a secret smile with Rachel.

"This afternoon we're going to—" Professor Stark was interrupted by a boy who tapped him on the shoulder.

"How do I find the website?" he asked.

"Look on the piece of paper for the

address," said Professor Stark.

"But where do I type the address?" the boy wailed.

Before Professor Stark could reply, a little girl darted up to him.

"What's a code block?" she asked.

"I thought you had done coding before," said Professor Stark.

"I have," said the girl, frowning. "I don't know why I'm finding it so hard."

Professor Stark went to help her, and Rachel and Kirsty exchanged a worried glance.

"This must be happening because the crafty calculator is missing," said Kirsty.

Rachel nodded. Cara had told them that without the crafty calculator, coders would get confused. They would forget simple things and muddle up the easiest tasks. Most of the other children were jabbing at their touch screens with one finger. Others were still trying to read the instructions.

"Everyone's confused," said Kirsty.

"Everyone except them," said Rachel.

She nodded over to where a couple of boys were leaning over their keyboard. A few people were standing behind them, looking impressed at what they were

doing. The boys were wearing caps pulled low over their faces.

"Let's go and see what they're working on," said Rachel.

They joined the group of children and peered over their shoulders.

"Oh my goodness," said Kirsty in shock. "Oh, no."

A cartoon figure of Jack Frost was doing a pirouette on the screen. Everyone giggled as he pranced around. Rachel and Kirsty stared at the boys. Under their caps, they had pointy chins, thin smiles and green skin.

"They're goblins," Rachel whispered. "What are they doing here?"

Chapter Seven
Locked Out

Before the girls could move, one of the goblins turned around and looked straight at Rachel. A look of alarm crossed his face. He dragged the other goblin off his stool and they scooted towards the back of the hall.

In a flash, Rachel and Kirsty were chasing them. They weaved around

crowds of people and glimpsed the
goblins disappearing through a doorway.

"This way," said Kirsty, hurrying after
the goblins.

The best friends found themselves
standing in a stairwell. The goblins were
nowhere to be seen.

"Which way do you think we should
go?" Rachel asked. "Up or down?"

"Shh," said Kirsty. "Listen."

Someone with large feet was thumping down the steps below. Rachel and Kirsty raced after them. At the bottom of the stairs was a door labelled 'Basement'.

"They must have gone in here," said Rachel.

She pushed the door open and peeped inside. The basement was dimly lit and there was a musty smell in the air. Rachel could see rows of tall shelves filled with dusty boxes.

"Look," Kirsty whispered. She pointed at two clear

sets of goblin footprints in the dust.

"It'll be easy to find them," said Rachel in a low voice. "We just have to follow the footprints."

The trail of prints led them through the rows of shelves towards the back of the basement. Glancing at the shelves, they could see that the boxes were filled with old computer equipment. In a few places, the footprints were scuffed where the goblins had squabbled and pushed each other. At last, at the end of a row, the girls saw the goblins. They were standing in front of a laptop, banging on the keys.

"Stupid computers!" the shorter goblin shouted angrily.

"Look," said Kirsty again, pointing at the wall behind the goblins.

A little door appeared in the middle of

the wall. It was about a quarter of
the size of the girls, and it was ice blue.
The handle was shaped like a large bolt
of lightning.

"Let me do it, you idiot," squawked the
taller goblin, shoving him aside. "Jack
Frost said we have to press three numbers
to make it work."

He pressed his knobbly fingers on three keys, the laptop pinged, and the little door swung open.

"Oh!" said Kirsty in amazement.

"I did it," said the taller goblin, rubbing his hands together. "I'm so clever."

"Stop!" cried Rachel, stepping out from behind the shelves.

"Too late," the shorter goblin called in a singsong voice.

"You'll never get us, or this," said the taller goblin, sniggering.

He held up a sparkling silver calculator and waved it at the girls. They knew it must be the crafty calculator.

"That doesn't belong to you," said Kirsty. "Give it back."

"No way," the shorter goblin replied. "Jack Frost locked this door with a computer program. You will never be able to crack the secret code and get through."

Squawking with laughter, the goblins scrambled through the little door and slammed it shut behind them.

Chapter Eight
Cracking the Secret Code

Rachel and Kirsty raced over to the laptop. The goblins had left it open on a table.

"We have to follow them," said Rachel. "They said that the secret code was three numbers long."

She tried pressing 123, but the door didn't open.

"Just keep pressing numbers," said Kirsty. "Maybe we'll get lucky and find the secret code by accident."

"Two, four, six," said Rachel, tapping on the keys. "No. Three, six, nine. No."

Kirsty groaned. "This could take hours," she said. "Oh, Rachel – look!"

On a nearby shelf, one of the dusty boxes was glowing. As the girls watched, the box burst open and Cara fluttered out in a cloud of sparkles.

"Cara, your crafty calculator

is somewhere through that door," said Rachel. "Jack Frost has used a computer program to lock us out."

"The goblins said that you have to type in three numbers to make the door open," Kirsty added.

Cara swooped over to the computer and looked at the screen.

"This program was built with computer code," she said. "If we can work out how the code was designed, we can take it apart and open the door."

"My brain feels foggy every time I think about coding," said Rachel.

"That's because Jack Frost has my

crafty calculator," said Cara, hopping on to the number keys. "It's confusing coders everywhere. But if the three of us work together, maybe we can do it." She cartwheeled across the keyboard, and lines of code scrolled up the screen.

"Here's the code! But I can't understand it without the crafty calculator."

They all stared at the lines of code.

"I think the answer must be here, somewhere in the middle," said Kirsty, scrolling down. "Even if we've forgotten how to code, we should be able to look for the right words."

"It must be something to do with opening the door," said Cara. "The code will tell the door to open when certain numbers are pressed."

"There!" exclaimed Rachel, pointing. "It says 'unlock'. That must be it."

"But where are the numbers?" Cara asked, reading the line of code. "I can't see a single one."

Rachel and Kirsty read through the line of code again and again, but Cara was right. There were no numbers.

"That's odd," said Kirsty. "Those three letters are just sitting on their own. D I H. I wonder what they're for."

"Oh!" said Rachel. "I've heard that coders sometimes use variables to store numbers. Maybe those letters represent numbers?"

"That's it!" said Cara. "Maybe it's as simple as A is 1, B is 2, and so on. So if Jack Frost is using that code, the number would be 498. Let's give it a go!"

Quickly, she closed the coding screen and typed the numbers on the keyboard. At once, the laptop pinged and the little door swung open.

"We did it!" said Kirsty, hugging her best friend and jumping up and down.

They ran over to the door, and then

stopped. It was so small that they had to kneel down to peer through. All they could see was a long, dark tunnel.

"This is going to be a narrow squeak," said Rachel.

"Wait," said Cara with a smile. "It'll be a lot easier if you're the same size as me."

She waved her wand, and a shimmering
ribbon of fairy dust lit up the dingy
basement. It wrapped itself around the
girls in a big, sparkling bow, and at once
they felt themselves shrinking to fairy
size. Their wings fluttered, and the glitter
faded as they rose into the air.

"We're ready," said Kirsty, giving a twirl in mid-air. "Let's go and get that crafty calculator back!"

Chapter Nine
Goblins in Hiding

As soon as they had fluttered through the door, it closed behind them. The tunnel stretched out ahead. Cara made the tip of her wand glow like a torch.

"What is this place?" Rachel asked.

"I think it's a magical tunnel," said Cara. "I bet Jack Frost made it to hide my crafty calculator."

"I wonder where it goes," said Kirsty.

Eager to find out, the fairies flew along the tunnel in single file. After a few minutes, there was a faint sound ahead.

Cuckoo! Cuckoo!

"Did you hear that?" asked Rachel, astonished. "It sounded like a bird."

Exchanging curious glances, the fairies flew on. Soon they reached another door. Cara tapped the handle with her wand, and the door opened a crack. There was a sudden blast of cackling laughter. For a moment, the fairies thought that they had been captured. But no one came to grab them, and they peered out through.

They were outside a small room with a table in the middle. Three goblins in jeans and T-shirts were standing at the table with their backs to the door.

"That's strange," whispered Rachel.
"There are no windows."

Kirsty looked around and saw a cuckoo clock hanging high up on the wall.

"That's the bird we heard," she said. "Let's hide in the clock and see what's going on."

The goblins didn't turn around, so the fairies were able to slip inside the clock without being seen. The first thing they saw inside was a little blue cuckoo on a spring. They pushed open the cuckoo clock's door and looked down. Cara's crafty calculator was lying on the table, and the goblins were leaning over it.

"Work out how many toes we all have," a scruffy goblin was saying.

The tall goblin who had been at Funcode busily tapped some numbers into the calculator.

"Eleventy-seventy, five hundred and two," he said.

The second goblin from Funcode jumped up and down and clapped his bony hands together.

"How many minutes would it take to eat one hundred muffins?" he asked.

The tall goblin jabbed at the calculator again.

"Fifteen bajillion and a half," he said.

"How many socks to stop your feet being so stinky?" asked the scruffy goblin.

The short goblin exploded with

laughter, and the tall goblin blew him a loud raspberry.

"I'm bored of sitting around waiting for Jack Frost," he whined. "Why do we have to stay here?"

"Jack Frost wants us to keep the crafty calculator here," said the scruffy goblin. "He said we always end up letting the fairies get things, so this time he has made sure they can't."

Rachel, Kirsty and Cara looked at each other.

"We'll never get my crafty calculator from them," said Cara. "It's the only thing they have to play with."

"Don't give up," said Kirsty, squeezing Cara's hand. "We just have to think of a way to distract them."

"Cara, could you use your magic to change the clock?" asked Rachel suddenly. "I think I've got an idea."

Chapter Ten
Twelve Bongs

"What's your idea, Rachel?" asked Kirsty.

"I think that the goblins would be distracted if this were a goblin clock instead of a cuckoo clock," Rachel said with a smile.

Cara's eyes sparkled and she waved her

wand. Instantly, the little blue cuckoo was replaced by two tiny goblins. Cara tapped them with her wand and they started to hop and twirl.

"The clock's going to strike twelve bongs," she said. "Stand back."

There was a whirring noise and then the clock door popped open. The fairies darted out of the way, and the tiny goblins shot out through the door.

"SQUAWK! SQUAWK!" they said.

BONG! went the clock.

The real goblins looked up and the toy goblins started to dance.

"Look!" the tallest real goblin cried.

BONG! The goblins squealed and laughed as the toys danced around. They

copied the dance, leaping over the chairs and kicking up their legs. The toys linked arms and skipped in circles, and the goblins did the same.

BONG!

Kirsty looked at the table and gasped.

"The calculator's gone," she cried.

"One of them must have put it in his pocket," said Cara.

"And we've only got nine bongs to find it," said Rachel. "Come on!"

BONG! The fairies zoomed down to the capering goblins. Rachel dived into the first one's pocket and found only holes. *BONG!* She tumbled out through the bottom and followed Kirsty and Cara into the second pocket.

"Ugh, fluff and stink bombs," said Kirsty, clinging to the side of the pocket as the goblin jigged about. "It's not in here."

BONG! Rachel and Cara pulled

Kirsty into the next pocket. Sticky sweet wrappers stuck to their wings, and there was a whiff of rotten potatoes. *BONG!* Kirsty saw something shining under a pink whoopee cushion.

"I see it!" she cried in delight. *BONG!* She reached out for it, but the goblin gave a hop and the calculator slipped out of sight.

"Hold on to me," said Cara.

BONG! Rachel and Kirsty grabbed one of her hands, and she stretched her other hand after the calculator.

"Almost," Cara cried.

BONG! Rachel and Kirsty stretched as hard as they could, and the tips of Cara's fingers touched the calculator. Instantly, it shrank to fairy size.

BONG!

"That was number eleven," Kirsty exclaimed. "Let's go!"

They zoomed out of the smelly pocket towards the little door.

BONG!

The tiny goblins disappeared and became a cuckoo again. The real goblins looked around and saw the fairies.

"Stop them!" the shortest one cried out. "Shut the door!"

The fairies zipped through the doorway a second before the goblins reached it. With a tap of her wand, Cara shut and locked the door.

"We did it," she said.

The goblins' shrieks faded as the fairies flew back along the tunnel. Soon,

they were back in the basement of the conference centre. Cara returned Rachel and Kirsty to human size.

"Thank you," she said with a smile.

"Now there's just the nifty notebook left to find," said Kirsty.

"Do you think we can get it back?" Cara asked.

"We're a team," said Kirsty. "And we won't stop until we get all your magical objects back. We promise."

Story Three
The Nifty Notebook

Chapter Eleven
Coders in a Pickle

Cara slipped into Kirsty's pocket and the girls hurried back to the conference centre.

"Hopefully things should be a bit calmer now that we've found the crafty calculator and the lucky laptop," said Rachel.

Kirsty pushed open the door to the

conference centre, and what she saw stopped her in her tracks.

"I think you might have spoken too soon," she said.

The hall looked busier and more confusing than ever. Books, bits of paper and bags were being scattered left and right as people hurried along.

"I can't find my watch," one girl muttered as she ran past.

"I know it sounds silly but I seem to have forgotten my name," said a man in a tweed jacket.

"Which way is the hub?" asked a boy who was standing right in front of it.

"My diary is missing," another boy was wailing.

"Where is my next class?" a teacher was asking anyone who would listen.

"What am I doing here?" a bearded man cried out.

"Oh my goodness," said Rachel. "What's happening?"

They stepped back into the stairwell and Cara fluttered out of Kirsty's pocket.

"This is happening because my nifty notebook is missing," she said. "It helps coders stay organised, which is super important. Coding can be really complicated, and coders can get into a real pickle if they don't keep on top of what they're doing."

Rachel and Kirsty exchanged a worried glance.

"We have to find that notebook before everyone at the conference goes completely scatterbrained," said Kirsty.

"But where should we start looking for it?" asked Cara. "Here or in Fairyland?"

Rachel thought for a moment. "Queen Titania always says that we should let the magic come to us," she said. "Maybe we should just join a class and see what happens."

"But what if the nifty notebook isn't here?" asked Cara. "We could be wasting our time and making things worse."

"Let's split up," said Kirsty. "Rachel and I will stay here and keep watch for goblins, while you go back to Fairyland and see if you can find anything out."

"Good idea," said Cara. "I'll ask the queen to look into her Seeing Pool to try

to find the nifty notebook."

She twirled into the air and was gone in a flurry of sparkling fairy dust. Rachel and Kirsty looked at each other.

"If the magic's going to find us, I hope it happens soon," said Rachel.

"Let's go and join the Design a Game class," Kirsty suggested. "And don't forget to keep a lookout for goblins!"

Chapter Twelve
An Ink-and-Paper Queen

By the time the girls arrived at the class, it was almost full. They took the last seats right at the back and pulled out their laptops. Everyone in the class seemed to be talking at the same time, and pieces of paper, tablets, pens and mobile phones were being dropped all around them.

"It's chaos," murmured Rachel.

"Please follow the instructions on
the piece of paper in front of you," the
teacher was bellowing over the racket.

"All the instructions are in the wrong
order," complained one boy.

"Mine's written in French," called out a
girl. "I don't speak French."

Kirsty picked up the piece of paper in

front of her and frowned.

"These aren't proper words," she said. "It's just gobbledygook. Oh my goodness, what's happening?"

As she was staring at the nonsense words, they started to swirl around on the paper. The black lines stopped looking like words at all. Kirsty and Rachel stared as the lines joined together and made a shape …
a very familiar shape …

"It's Queen Titania," Rachel whispered in excitement.

The ink-and-paper queen beckoned to them

with one slender finger. At once, the girls
felt as if something was dragging them
forwards. Then, in the blink of an eye,
they were pulled headfirst into the paper.

For a moment, the girls were
surrounded by a whirl of black and
white. Then they felt themselves shooting

upwards, and they burst through something that glimmered and splashed around them. Gasping and spluttering, they found themselves standing beside the Fairyland seeing pool, with their gossamer wings fluttering behind them. Queen Titania and Cara were standing

opposite the two friends.

"Welcome to Fairyland, Kirsty and
Rachel," said Queen Titania.

The girls quickly curtsied.

"Thank you, Your Majesty," said
Rachel. "I hope that we weren't seen."

"The humans didn't see anything,"
said the queen with a smile. "I'm sorry it
was so sudden, but this is urgent.
Jack Frost has sneaked into the royal
computer room."

"We don't know what he's doing,"
said Cara. "But we're sure it's something
naughty. Will you come with me to
find out?"

Rachel and Kirsty agreed at once,
and Cara led them into the castle. The
frog footman bowed to the fairies as
they hurried past.

"Hello, Bertram," they called.

"Welcome back to Fairyland," he said. "Have you come to get Jack Frost out of the castle?"

"We're going to try," said Rachel as they hurried on.

"What do you think Jack Frost is doing in the computer room?" Kirsty asked. "Is he trying to steal something?"

"There's nothing there except the royal computer," said Cara.

They reached the computer room door and peered inside. Jack Frost was sitting hunched over in front of a sparkling computer, tapping at the keyboard. A notebook was lying on the desk beside him.

"That's it," Cara whispered in a worried voice. "My nifty notebook."

"Let's try to creep up behind him," Rachel suggested. "He's so interested in what he's doing, we might be able to grab the notebook before he notices us."

Chapter Thirteen
Frost in a Fury

Cara, Rachel and Kirsty tiptoed across the polished floor towards the computer. Cara rose into the air and stretched her hand out towards the nifty notebook ...

"NO!"

Jack Frost whirled around and his hand slammed down on top of the notebook.

Rachel and Kirsty jumped and pulled Cara back. Jack Frost glowered at the Coding Fairy.

"You," he said, pointing a long, bony finger at her. "What have you done? Why isn't my coding working? Tell me!"

"Give me my notebook back," Cara demanded. "I won't help you with

anything until you do."

"It's mine now," Jack Frost hissed. "Listen, you pest. I've got everything organised. I know exactly what I want to do and what order to do it in. So why isn't it working?"

He thumped the desk again, and the computer jumped into the air.

Cara folded her arms and frowned at him.

"My notebook won't help you to be a coder," she said. "It will only help you to be more organised. I can teach you how to code. But I won't help you as long as you have my notebook."

Rachel and Kirsty looked at Jack Frost
and Cara. Neither of them was willing to
give in. Kirsty took a step forward.

"What do you want your app to do?"
she asked Jack Frost.

"It's not just an app," said Jack Frost.
"It's a game. The best game ever, starring
me, me, ME!"

"What happens in this game, exactly?"
asked Rachel.

"None of your business," said Jack Frost. "All you need to know is that I always win, and it's brilliant."

"Except that it's not working, is it?" said Cara.

"You need Cara's help," said Rachel. "Give her the nifty notebook and she'll help you."

"Never!" cried Jack Frost.

He disappeared in a flash of blue lightning, taking the nifty notebook with him.

"No!" cried Cara.

She sank down on the ground and buried her face in her hands. Kirsty bent down beside her.

"We'll get your notebook back, I promise," she said.

"But how?" Cara said, sniffing.

Rachel smiled.

"By giving him exactly what he wants," she said. "We're going to let him beat us. Jack Frost is going to win."

Chapter Fourteen
An Icy Welcome

Kirsty and Cara stared at Rachel in astonishment. She laughed.

"Trust me," she said. "If we can build this game for Jack Frost, he'll give us the nifty notebook in return. He won't be able to resist if he can see a game where he's the winner."

"You're right," said Kirsty, jumping to her feet. "People love using coding to build virtual worlds. If we build a virtual world where Jack Frost can defeat Cara, maybe he'll leave her alone in the real world."

Cara's eyes started to sparkle again.

"It's worth a try," she said, smiling. "Let's get started."

She waved her wand, and three mugs of steaming hot chocolate appeared on the desk, together with a plate of biscuits. Grinning, Rachel and Kirsty sat down beside her.

They started by working on separate pieces of code. Rachel designed the backgrounds, Cara invented the characters and Kirsty developed the movements and the actions. Then they

put everything together and started to come up with story ideas. Turning their ideas into code, they created adventures for Jack Frost that would make him feel like the star of the show. They gave him heroic poses and brave words. They made him clever and popular. Coding block by coding block, they built him a world where he was the hero.

At last, Kirsty rubbed her eyes and Rachel yawned and stretched. "That's it," said Cara. "We've done everything we can. The *Jack Frost Adventures* game is finished."

They loaded the game on to a tablet and set off for the Ice Castle. Soon the green gardens and bright colours of the fairy homes faded, and the sky grew grim and grey. They saw a few feeble lights in Goblin Grotto, which lay in the cold shadow of the Ice Castle. Cara shivered.

"Should we knock on the castle door?" she whispered.

"No," said Rachel. "We have to be
bold. Let's rap on the window of the
throne room."

She and Kirsty had visited the castle
many times, so they knew where to
find the throne room. They perched on
the wide stone windowsill and knocked
sharply on the glass.

"Stop those birds pecking the windows!" Jack Frost yelled from inside.

A goblin flung the window open, and gave a squawk of surprise when he saw the fairies. They fluttered in before he could say a word. Several goblin servants were lounging around the room. Jack Frost was sprawling on his throne, but he jumped up when he saw the fairies.

"Get them!" he yelled at the goblins.

Chapter Fifteen
A Perfect Game

"Lock them in the dungeons!" Jack
Frost screeched. "Tie them up! Feed
them stale crusts!"

Kirsty held up her hand.

"Just a minute," she said. "Aren't you
wondering why we're here?"

Jack Frost's eyes narrowed.

"We've brought something to show you," said Cara.

Rachel held up the tablet and started to play the demo of *The Jack Frost Adventures*. Jack Frost stared. His eyes widened. His mouth fell open. As soon as the demo ended, he thrust out his hand.

"Give it to me!" he demanded.

"Not until you give Cara her notebook back," said Rachel.

"Fools!" Jack Frost shouted. "My goblins will take it from you and lock you up."

"They could do that," Kirsty agreed. "But you would only have the demo of the game."

"We'll send you the full game as soon as we're safely back at my computer lab with my notebook," Cara added.

Jack Frost went purple, then red, and then white with fury. Then he pulled the notebook from inside his clock and flung it at Cara. She caught it and hugged it to her chest.

"Give me my game," Jack Frost growled angrily.

Rachel fluttered forwards and gently placed the tablet into his hands. He snatched it and started to play the demo

again. The goblins
gathered around
him to watch, and
he glanced up at the
fairies.

"What are you
waiting for?" he
snapped. "Scram!"

A short time later, Rachel, Kirsty and
Cara were standing before Queen Titania
in the Fairyland palace throne room.

"So Jack Frost has his new game, and
Cara's magical objects are safely back
where they belong," said the queen.
"Rachel and Kirsty, once again you have
helped save the magic of the fairies. How
can we ever thank you?"

"There's no need," said Kirsty. "We're just happy to have been able to help."

"I think things will be peaceful for quite a while," added Rachel. "While Jack Frost is busy defeating the fairies in his game world, he'll leave you all alone in real life!"

Cara laughed and hugged Rachel and Kirsty.

"I've really enjoyed getting to know you both," she said. "But now I think it's time that you went back to Funcode. There are still lots of amazing classes for you to attend – and now that my magical objects are back where they belong, everything will run smoothly."

"Goodbye, and thank you again," said the queen.

As she spoke, the throne room started

to fade, and her words echoed as if she were speaking from far away. For a moment, all Rachel and Kirsty could see was a flurry of tiny sparkles. They blinked, and found themselves sitting at the back of the coding class with their laptops open in front of them. This time, the instructions on the paper they were holding made perfect sense.

"How to Design a Game," Kirsty read out. "Step one, choose a title …"

The best friends shared a happy smile.

"I've got the perfect name," said Rachel. "*Fun in Fairyland!*"

The End

**Now it's time for Kirsty and
Rachel to help …**

Evelyn the
Mermicorn
Fairy

"I love listening to the rain beating
on the window," said Rachel Walker.
"Especially when it's so cosy inside."

She snuggled deeper into her favourite
armchair and gazed into the flickering
flames of the fire. Her best friend, Kirsty
Tate, put down the pattern she was
stitching.

"Me too," she said.

Kirsty was spending the last week of
the summer holidays at Rachel's house
in Tippington. Although they went to

different schools, they saw each other
as often as they could. They always had
the best fun when they were together,
and they often shared secret, magical
adventures with their fairy friends.

The sitting room door opened and
Rachel's dad popped his head around it.

"Anyone for hot chocolate?" he asked.

"Yes please," said the girls together.

"With whipped cream and sprinkles?"
Rachel added.

"Of course," said Mr Walker. "Maybe
it'll make up for not being able to go
pebble collecting on the beach. What did
you want the pebbles for?"

"We were going to paint inspiring
pictures and messages on them, and then
put them back on the beach for other
people to find," Kirsty explained.

"But it's OK," said Rachel. "We found

something else crafty to do instead."

Her dad looked at the cross-stitch patterns they were holding. Kirsty was working on a turquoise mermaid with golden hair, and Rachel was stitching a snow-white unicorn.

"Those look complicated," he said.

"Yes, but it'll be a great feeling when they're finished," said Kirsty.

Mr Walker went to make the hot chocolate, and the girls carried on stitching.

"What's your favourite, mermaids or unicorns?" asked Rachel.

"I don't think I can choose," said Kirsty. "After all, we've met them both on our adventures, and they were just as magical and inspiring as each other."

Just then, they heard a tiny, tinkling giggle. The girls exchanged a surprised glance.

"That sounded exactly like a fairy," said Rachel.

There was another bell-like giggle, and the girls jumped to their feet.

"Where are you?" Kirsty asked.

Then Rachel noticed that her dark hair was sprinkled with sparkling fairy dust. Kirsty saw the same thing on Rachel's hair. They both looked up at the same time, and laughed out loud.

A chestnut-haired fairy was waving at them from the top of the round glass light pendant. She slid down it with a whoop and turned somersaults through the air, landing on the sofa arm with a bounce. She was wearing a shimmering, glittery blue skirt and a matching denim jacket.

"Hello," she said. "I'm Evelyn the Mermicorn Fairy."

"Hello, Evelyn," said Rachel, kneeling

down in front of her. "What has brought you to my sitting room?"

"And what's a mermicorn?" Kirsty added.

"Exactly what it sounds like," said Evelyn with a smile. "It's the rarest, most magical creature in all of Fairyland — half mermaid and half unicorn."

"Oh, it sounds wonderful," said Kirsty in a whisper. "I wish I could see one."

"We only see them once a year," said Evelyn. "We always celebrate their visit with the Mermicorn Festival. That's why I'm here. Would you like to come and enjoy the festival with me?"

Rachel and Kirsty squealed in excitement.

"We'd love to," said Kirsty.

"Then it's time to go to Fairyland," said Evelyn. She opened her hand, and the girls saw that she was holding a little pile of sparkling fairy dust.

"Don't you have a wand?" asked Rachel.

Evelyn smiled.

"Not today," she said.

She blew the fairy dust towards the girls, and a pastel rainbow swirled around them. Everything shimmered in light shades of blue, yellow, green and pink. Rachel and Kirsty reached for each other's hand as their delicate wings unfolded.

"Listen," said Kirsty. "The rain sounds different."

"Yes, I can't hear the raindrops spattering against the window any more," said Rachel. "It sounds more like … waves."

At that moment, the pastel-coloured

swirl of fairy dust vanished away, and the girls found themselves sitting on a small stretch of golden sand.

"It *was* waves," said Kirsty in delight. "Yippee, we made it to the beach after all."

"This is a bit more magical than the one I was planning to visit," said Rachel with a happy laugh.

"Welcome to Mermicorn Island," said Evelyn.

"I've never seen such fine sand," said Kirsty, letting it run through her fingers.

"Or such blue sea," Rachel added, cartwheeling down to the shore.

The sun was sparkling on the water, and it looked as if tiny diamonds were dancing in the waves. As Rachel turned around to smile at her best friend, she saw a beautiful sight. At the edge of the beach was a row of candy-coloured stalls, gleaming with a pearly sheen. Fairies were walking barefoot from stall to stall, wearing shells plaited into their hair and pearls threaded into necklaces and belts. The Music Fairies were playing an oceanic tune on driftwood instruments.

"I can taste the salt in the air," said Kirsty, taking a deep breath.

"What happens at the Mermicorn Festival?" Rachel asked.

"Music, dancing, good food, good fun," said Evelyn, spinning around with her arms held wide. "It's my favourite time of year."

Just then, Shannon the Ocean Fairy came dancing across the sand towards them.

"Rachel and Kirsty!" she cried, giving them a hug. "It's great to see you. Evelyn, when will the mermicorns be here? I can't wait to see them."

"Very soon," said Evelyn. "Let's get everyone to come down to the shore."

"Why is everyone walking?" asked Rachel, as they watched their fairy friends moving down to the shore.

"Because even fairies like to feel the sand between our toes sometimes," said Evelyn, smiling. "We all leave our wands at the palace when we come here. We agreed that Mermicorn Island should only be for mermicorn magic."

Just then, the music changed. It was as gentle and flowing as the waves. The shallow, clear water began to swirl around in a whirlpool.

"Wow, the water's changing colour," said Kirsty.

The whirlpool had turned a lighter,

more sparkling blue, and seemed to be lit by a light from below.

"Something's coming out of it," said Rachel, tingling all over with excitement.

Rachel and Kirsty watched as a spiral horn rose up through the swirling water. The head and neck of a beautiful unicorn appeared. Three colourful gemstones hung around her neck on a golden chain. Then a sparkling green mermaid tail flicked out of the water. The fairies cheered and waved, and the mermicorn bowed its head. Evelyn waded out to the whirlpool and reached out her hand.

"This is Topaz," said Evelyn.

She let her hand rest on Topaz's mane for a moment. Rachel and Kirsty did the same thing, and at once a strong feeling of confidence flooded through them.

At the same time, the gems Topaz was wearing glowed even more brightly.

"How funny," said Kirsty. "I've been feeling worried about the homework project I chose to do for school, but all of a sudden I feel certain that I picked the right one."

Evelyn smiled. "Topaz's magic is working," she said. "You see, the gems that she wears have the power to make everyone around them feel confident. Her blue gem gives you confidence in your own choices and ideas. Her pink gem gives you confidence to speak your mind, and helps you be brave enough to stand up for the things you believe in. And the green gemstone gives you the confidence to advise others."

Just then, several other mermicorns broke through the foaming waters, each with a different-coloured tail. The other fairies were all in the water now, and they started to play with the mermicorns, stroking their manes, laughing and singing. The mermicorns were leaping through the foamy waves, flicking their tails. Topaz stayed close to Evelyn, nuzzling close, with love in her big, shining eyes.

"What an amazing sight," said Rachel, looking around in wonder at the fairies and mermicorns.

Read Evelyn the Mermicorn Fairy to find out what adventures are in store for Kirsty and Rachel!

Calling all parents, carers and teachers!
The Rainbow Magic fairies are here to help
your child enter the magical world of reading.
Whatever reading stage they are at, there's
a Rainbow Magic book for everyone!
Here is Lydia the Reading Fairy's guide to
supporting your child's journey at all levels.

Starting Out

(1)

Our Rainbow Magic Beginner Readers are perfect for first-time readers who are just beginning to develop reading skills and confidence. Approved by teachers, they contain a full range of educational levelling, as well as lively full-colour illustrations.

Developing Readers

(2)

Rainbow Magic Early Readers contain longer stories and wider vocabulary for building stamina and growing confidence. These are adaptations of our most popular Rainbow Magic stories, specially developed for younger readers in conjunction with an Early Years reading consultant, with full-colour illustrations.

Going Solo

(3)

The Rainbow Magic chapter books – a mixture of series and one-off specials – contain accessible writing to encourage your child to venture into reading independently. These highly collectible and much-loved magical stories inspire a love of reading to last a lifetime.

www.rainbowmagicbooks.co.uk

"Rainbow Magic got my daughter reading chapter books. Great sparkly covers, cute fairies and traditional stories full of magic that she found impossible to put down" – Mother of Edie (6 years)

"Florence LOVES the Rainbow Magic books. She really enjoys reading now" – Mother of Florence (6 years)

The Rainbow Magic
Reading Challenge

Well done, fairy friend – you have completed the book!
This book was worth 10 points.

See how far you have climbed on the
Reading Rainbow opposite.

The more books you read, the more points you will get,
and the closer you will be to becoming a Fairy Princess!

Do you want your own Reading Rainbow?
1. Cut out the coin below
2. Go to the Rainbow Magic website
3. Download and print out your poster
4. Add your coin and climb up the Reading Rainbow!

There's all this and lots more at
www.rainbowmagicbooks.co.uk

You'll find activities, competitions, stories, a special
newsletter and complete profiles of all the
Rainbow Magic fairies. Find a fairy with your name!